BREAKOUT

A MICHAEL QUINN SHORT STORY

Kevin Scott Olson

Prisión Federal Norte Baja,
Mexico

"YOU WANT TO EAT TONIGHT, *GRINGO?*"
The prison guard lifted the plastic bowl off the tray and laid the tray on the floor. He held the bowl out in front of him, displaying its contents, a watery brown liquid with a few beans floating on top.

"You can have your dinner. All it takes is a little *mordida*. A little of this." The guard made a folding-money motion, rubbing his thumb against the fingers of his free hand. His pockmarked brown face creased into a yellow-toothed smile.

The prisoner sat, hunched over, on the edge of his bunk. He glanced at the bowl, then stared at the concrete floor of his cell and spoke softly. "Already told you boys. Ain't got no more money."

The black-uniformed guard sighed. His smile disappeared, and he glanced at the guard standing next to him. The other guard shrugged his shoulders and silently chewed his toothpick, one hand resting on the butt of his holstered pistol.

"That is not good for you, my friend. No, not good." The prison guard gestured at the cramped cell, whose sole furnishings were a filth-encrusted open toilet, a sink, and a metal bunk. "You can have better than this. Everything you might want, it is for sale in this prison.

"You want a cell with a window? Maybe pizza? Drugs? A pretty *puta* to keep you company at night? You have money, you can have all those things.

"But with no money… " The guard bent over, holding the bowl level with the prisoner's face. He stared until the prisoner looked up and made eye contact. Then the guard hawked and spat into the bowl.

"You get this." The guard tilted the bowl so that the brown liquid poured onto the prisoner's shoes.

"Damn you!" The prisoner's manacled right fist lashed out, landing a solid uppercut to the guard's jaw. The bowl flew across the room, and the guard grunted and staggered back until he collided with the cell bars. He grabbed a bar and steadied himself.

Blood dripped from the guard's split lip. He cursed in Spanish as he felt his jaw and licked the blood away. With his thumb, he motioned for the other guard to stand lookout at the bars. Then he moved to the center of the cell.

"That was a big mistake, my friend. You *norteamericanos*, you never understand how things work down here."

The guard unclipped his baton from his duty belt. He rolled up his shirtsleeves, revealing the prominent tattoo of a black scorpion on his forearm.

"Now you get a lesson."

• • •

Pueblo de Pescado,
Mexico

The murder of black crows, its agitated *"caw-caw"* calls echoing back and forth in annoying concert, circled slowly in the burnt-orange sky of sunset.

Michael Quinn focused his binoculars until he could see the birds' feathers fluttering in the wind. Other than the noise of the birds, he was surrounded by silence. The rubbish-strewn room of the abandoned hotel was a good spot for recon, even with its musty stench and late-afternoon heat. The hotel was in a deserted area of vacant, crumbling old buildings, and the top-floor room's open window gave him a panoramic view.

Why had the word "murder" been assigned to describe such an innocuous group of birds? Yes, these crows were on the hunt, looking for their dinner, and hunting involved killing. But crows were probably always on the hunt. As were all animals. As were all living things.

He tilted the binoculars down and scanned the bird's hunting ground.

The sprawling compound of the *Prisión Federal Norte Baja* would be a reliable source of nourishment. Scraps of bread or meat always littered the grimy asphalt prison yards. And the end of the day, when the outdoor areas were largely empty, was a good time to go foraging for food.

A half dozen crows broke away from the rest, swooping down towards a trash can topped by a ripped paper bag that held the remnants of someone's meal.

"Now." Quinn spoke into the microphone of his earpiece. He leaned forward in his chair and tightened his grip on the binoculars.

Another crow broke away from the rest. It flapped its wings and flew in a smooth downwards arc toward the trash can. In the hazy sunset, the solitary crow looked very much like the others.

But this crow's eyes were camera lenses, its wings were black carbon fiber, its heartbeat electronic impulses.

Quinn tapped an icon on the tablet computer next to him and entered the encryption code. The app opened to reveal the drone's video feed—a high-resolution aerial view of the prison grounds. The trash can loomed large on the screen as the drone dove down.

"Got the feed." Quinn used his thumb and finger to adjust the tablet image. "Bring the bird back up and over the target cell."

The drone flapped its wings and flew away from the trash can, toward a squalid one-story concrete building in a corner of the compound. It circled over a section of the flat rooftop.

"That entire building is solitary." The voice of Will, Quinn's field supervisor, crackled in his earpiece. "Your man's cell is directly under the bird. Third cell in from that side entrance with the dirt courtyard."

"Bring the bird up over the entire compound. Let's see what we're dealing with."

The drone flew back up to join the circling crows, then leveled out and began a long, lazy loop around the perimeter of the prison complex.

Quinn put down the binoculars and picked up the tablet, scrutinizing the aerial view.

The notorious maximum-security *Prisión Federal*, known by locals as the *guarida del diablo*, the devil's lair, appeared pretty much like it did in the photographs: a compound of dingy gray buildings, interspersed with asphalt yards and a parking lot. It was surrounded by a fifteen-foot concrete wall topped with barbed wire and, at regular intervals, alarm horns.

All of the buildings were built of thick-walled concrete. Here and there the walls were chipped and cracked and sprayed with graffiti. The buildings looked as if they had been built fifty years ago, and hadn't been cleaned since.

The main entrance was a solid steel sliding door built into the concrete wall. Behind the door, eight black-clad guards holding rifles stood around or inside the guardhouse. Four guards with rifles stood in each of the watchtowers, the towers themselves concrete fortresses wrapped in double layers of barbed wire. Other guards, carrying shotguns and with holstered side arms on their hips, roamed the grounds in pairs.

"Will, you want me to get this guy out of there with zero collateral damage?"

"That's the goal."

"What did you have in mind? We can't helo in at night and fast-rope down to the roof. With the engine roar they'd be all over us. An operation like this would take fifteen, maybe twenty men. We'd have to hike in from a couple of miles away. Stage a predawn raid."

"Michael, relations with Mexico are shaky enough now. We can't risk having a group of American special ops forces captured assaulting a Mexican prison. It would be a nightmare of an international incident." Will paused, then continued. "We need someone who is totally off the books and who can get this done. That means you, my friend, flying solo. And soon. You know the high value of this asset. What you don't know is how precarious his situation is."

Quinn tapped another icon on his tablet. The screen shifted to a color photograph of an American soldier, dressed in camouflage clothes and holding a rifle. The brown-haired man looked to be in his mid-twenties. It was a bright sunny day, and the man was standing in front of a background of craggy brown mountains that Quinn guessed to be Afghanistan. The man stood about six foot three, broad-shouldered and bearded, and gazed stoically at the camera.

"I've heard of Bobby Devereaux. One of the best snipers in the SEALs. What can you tell me?"

Will's voice was guarded. "You already know that the Escorpiones drug cartel has been spreading aggressively into California and Texas. They've even taken over some border towns. Intel uncovered a plot to kidnap Americans for ransom. They're going to start by beheading a couple of Americans, just to let us know they're serious. Then settle into the kidnap-ransom routine as a long-term business plan. It's worked well for them elsewhere." Will's voice lowered. "The DEA and Homeland Security were getting nowhere. Covert action was needed. The decision was made to send in Devereaux to take out the Escorpiones' head guy."

"That's showing some stones."

"It would have sent the Escorpiones the message to not mess with the U.S. And, with a little creative assistance from us, it would have also ignited a turf war with a rival gang."

Quinn looked at the photo of the soldier. "From what I've heard about Devereaux, he likes to work alone. How was he going to get close to the target?"

"We have an informant inside the Escorpiones. He was going to tip us off as to the right time and place. Remember, Devereaux has taken out hostiles from up to a mile away. The opportunity would have arisen. You were right about him insisting on going alone. He made it across the border OK, just him in his pickup truck."

"What went wrong?"

"He was pulled over by the Mexican police. They said he was speeding, which was a crock. It was a shakedown, of course. But Devereaux hadn't brought enough cash to satisfy them. So, the police searched his truck. They found the hidden compartment in his truck bed, and there was his sniper rifle, a high-powered scope, and boxes of ammo." Will sighed. "That did it. The Mexican authorities went ballistic when they saw the sniper gear. Devereaux's been locked up in solitary for over two months now, still waiting for a hearing."

"Do the Mexicans know who he is?"

"His false ID is holding up so far. They didn't believe for a second his story about going out target shooting and making a wrong turn into Mexico, but they don't know who he really is. That's the only reason he's still alive."

Will's voice was somber. "But it's only a matter of time—days, maybe—until they find out. And any way it goes down, it's bad. If the Mexican government finds out who he is, then we are in the extremely awkward position of having sent an American assassin into a foreign country. Devereaux will get life in a Mexican hellhole. And if it's the Escorpiones that find out who he is—and for all we know, they run that damn prison—then he will simply disappear. And some cold morning his head will turn up on a Tijuana street corner."

Quinn cursed. His tightening gut always told him when a situation had no good options. He tapped the tablet screen, and the picture changed back to the video feed from the drone. "Will, bring that bird up higher. I want to see what's around this prison."

The drone flapped its wings and soared high above the crows, then curved into a long, graceful arc. Quinn looked at the aerial view on his tablet screen.

Like many prisons, the *Prisión Federal Norte Baja* was located outside of town, in a barren area where no one lived or would ever want to live. On each side of the prison walls was a football-field-sized chunk of land, with nothing but dirt and rocks. Past the land were a few industrial plants that, from their appearance, were so polluting and repulsive they too, along with the prison, had been exiled to the badlands.

Quinn looked them over carefully, searching for anything that might provide access to the prison.

On one side of the prison was a complex of four humble tin-roofed buildings arranged in a square. In the center of the square, lying on the dirt, was a large pile of animal bones and carrion. Quinn recognized horse and cow rib cages sticking up in the air. The place was a rendering plant.

On the other side of the prison was a larger, more modern-looking industrial plant with a maze of large pipes connecting steel cylindrical tanks and concrete buildings, interspersed with huge smokestacks. The tanker trucks in the parking lot confirmed that this was some sort of chemical plant. The brightly colored pictures of produce on the sides of the trucks indicated a food-processing business.

The businesses further out were more of the same— enterprises that no one wanted around. A decrepit complex of wood buildings with large tubs of dirty liquids and piles of animal hides lying on the ground; a tannery. A large lot that looked like a sea of old metal glinting in the sun, interspersed with patches of rust and piles of dirty tires; a wrecking yard.

All of the businesses were surrounded by chain link fences topped with barbed wire. They all undoubtedly had their own alarm systems. Above them the concentration of multiple pollutants had turned the sky into a permanent brown haze that shrouded everything in gloom.

This entire area was the *guarida del diablo.*

"Will, there's got to be another way. Get the State Department involved, call a meeting, exert some diplomatic pressure."

"We already have." The frustration was evident in Will's voice. "And we are getting stonewalled. Don't know precisely why, but I'm sure Devereaux's sniper gear set off alarms that went to the top of the Mexican government."

"Then go to the bottom. Money changes hands. The charges are dropped. Devereaux is quietly escorted out in the middle of the night."

"We tried that in the very beginning." Will's voice rose. "We got squat. This stone wall is solid from the bottom to the top."

"Will, you've got to have a Plan B."

"We do, Michael." Will took a breath and lowered his voice. "Our Plan B is you."

● ● ●

Washington, D.C.

"Let me assure you once again, Mr. Jenkins."

The man from the office of the Mexican SRE, the *Secretaria de Relaciones Exteriores,* spoke with the practiced patience of the diplomat. "The American's rights as a foreign national are being completely respected. He will have his right to due process. He will have a fair hearing."

The Mexican official paused for a sip from his glass of ice water, then placed his brown hands palms down on the mahogany conference table, next to his laptop. His broad shoulders filled out the well-cut, navy pinstripe suit, and his head of jet-black hair glistened in the fluorescent light of the drop ceiling. The bronze skin of his face was unlined for someone in early middle age, and he looked cool and comfortable in the air-conditioned room.

"And my country appreciates that, Mr. Hernandez." Jenkins kept his voice equally modulated. He glanced down at his pale hands. In comparison to the skin of the Mexican official, they looked the color of alabaster. His pale bald head probably looked like a cue ball in the fluorescent lights. Glancing at his laptop, he resisted the urge to drum his fingers on the conference table. "What we are asking for is your cooperation in the expedition of this matter, so that the American can be released in a timely fashion and return home to the United States."

The Mexican official raised his hands off of the table, and faced the palms toward the American. "Let me be clear, Mr. Jenkins. We will do what we can to help. We can speak again to the office of the Mexican

Attorney General. We can speak again to the office of the Governor of Baja California. We can ask them to do what they can to facilitate the processes of the *burocracia.*

"But what we cannot do"—the raised palms moved slightly forward in emphasis—"is in any way circumvent our laws. This American was caught in our country with"—the official glanced at his laptop screen—"a Desert Tactical SRS 'bullpup' rifle, a suppressor, a high-powered Leupold riflescope, and considerable quantities of Lapua .338 match-grade ammunition. In our country, the possession alone of such things is a very serious offense, a Federal offense. One that may result in years in prison.

"And this American, his past, or lack thereof, it seems to raise questions. It is correct, as you pointed out, that he has no criminal record. It is also correct that there is not much record of anything about this man, other than employment as an insurance claims processor. Such a man has never served in the military, but decides to carry around the equipment of a trained soldier?

"You know that in our country, as in your country, ignorance of the law is no excuse. We are a democracy, a nation of laws, like your country. And we must uphold our laws. Surely you have no reason to think otherwise?" The Mexican official laid his palms back on the table and leaned back in his chair.

"Of course not, Mr. Hernandez." Jenkins forced a reassuring smile and, replicating his counterpart's body language, sat back in his chair.

Oh, I don't know why we would think otherwise, Jenkins thought to himself. *Perhaps because huge chunks of your country are a frigging lawless narco-state, run by warring drug cartels that torture and murder at will?* He picked up his glass of ice water and drank, allowing himself a few extra seconds to confirm what he had already decided, that it was time to bring in the big guns. The back of his shirt collar was damp with sweat. As he put the glass down, he put the smile back on his face.

"We fully understand, Mr. Hernandez. You must work within your own legal system. We respect that." Jenkins cleared his throat. *Careful now.* "It's just that we do not want this to escalate into any kind of diplomatic conflict. Conflict that could have political ramifications with regard to the tariffs currently under re-negotiation. Conflict that could decrease popular support for the substantial aid our country continues to provide to your country." *Better stop there.* He kept the smile on his face and waited.

For a moment, the Mexican official's dark eyes glittered with what may have been anger. Then the moment passed, and the eyes showed only resignation, boredom at having to be where he was when there were so many more important matters to be handled elsewhere. He spoke with a quiet finality. "I have my superiors to answer to, as do you, Mr. Jenkins. And we wish to do nothing to endanger your government's very generous support." The official closed his laptop and stood, pushing back his chair. "You must now excuse me. I have another appointment for which I am behind schedule." He placed the laptop in his briefcase.

"When can we meet again?" Jenkins felt the cold sweat against the back of his neck.

"When we have something new to discuss." The Mexican official turned and opened the door to the hallway. He stopped in the doorway and turned back, as if realizing he had been flippant. "I mean to say, when we have progress on this matter. Perhaps when this American has his court hearing? That should not be long. No more than a month or two from now." He turned and walked out of the room.

Jenkins sat back in his chair and sighed. He had so much more on his plate than this case. But he had to do whatever he could. The cell phone in his inside coat pocket vibrated. He removed it and looked at the screen.

Status? read the encrypted text.

He tapped the keys, his reply not bothering with diplomatic niceties. *Status is we are still being jerked around. Zero. Nada. If you have Plan B, recommend you pull trigger.*

• • •

Breakout

Three days later
La Encantada Hotel
Pueblo de Pescado,
Mexico

With any operation, the waiting was the hardest part.

The best ops were simple and quick. Simple, because things always changed. Quick, because each individual step had been drilled into muscle memory. Sketch it out, review carefully once or twice, and then fifteen minutes later get'er done.

The operation he was about to execute met none of those criteria.

At his corner table in the hotel bar, Quinn stared at the bottle of Negra Modelo he was pretending to drink. Though he had been up all night, the pills he had taken at dawn still had him wired. He absent-mindedly scratched the day-old stubble on his chin. In his mind, he checked and rechecked his gear again, then ran through the operation for what seemed like the hundredth time. There was no escaping the fact that this plan could go wrong in countless ways.

When there were hours to kill before an operation, time was not his friend. His mind dreamt up unrealistic contingencies. Bizarre worst-case scenarios appeared that were extremely unlikely—but just possible enough to rattle him. These scenarios lurked in the corners of his mind like ghosts.

He forced his eyes away from the beer and glanced around the room. The hotel bar was getting crowded as late Friday afternoon segued into the evening mix of tourists and locals.

This place was the right spot for killing time. Large and stylish enough to be popular. Yet casual enough for him—in his T-shirt, Crye pants, and hiking boots—to blend in as just another weekend warrior, down in Mexico to have a little fun in the desert.

The happy-hour buzz of conversation faded into the background as his gaze shifted to the window behind the bar. From his corner table, he could see the alley behind the hotel and the stained, discarded blanket which partly hung off the dumpster and fully covered up his motorcycle.

What had he heard about this Bobby Devereaux? Not much. Country boy. Quiet, polite. Kept to himself.

What sort of miserable cell was Devereaux stuck in? The battles between the drug cartels were only getting worse. Would Mexico someday collapse into the equivalent of a Somalia, a failed state run by warlords?

"Excuse me, *señor.*"

A whiff of spicy perfume accompanied the feminine voice. From behind him, his cocktail waitress placed a new chilled bottle of Negra Modelo on his table.

"I brought you a new *cerveza* since —ah, you have scarcely touched the first one. I will take this one back?"

"It's OK, *señorita.* You can leave the new bottle and take the old. I like my beer cold." Quinn looked down at his table and didn't say anything more. He hadn't paid any attention to her when he had ordered his drink, and wasn't going to start now. It was important to stay anonymous.

"Of course, *señor.*" The waitress leaned in and picked up the old bottle. As she did so the bar rag on her drink tray slipped off and fell forward, onto the floor underneath Quinn's table.

"*Lo siento.*" Before Quinn could react, the waitress stepped forward and bent over next to the table to reach down and pick up the rag. As she did, her thigh bumped the table and the ends of her long mane of coal-black hair spilled over onto Quinn's forearm. His skin tingled at the touch, and for a second he just stared at the shiny luster of the beautiful black hair resting on his forearm. Her spicy perfume was stronger, and had a touch of some kind of exotic fruit.

He suddenly realized that her torso was only inches to the left of his face. The waitress grunted as she stretched under the table to reach the rag, which had landed close to the wall. As she bent over further her short, black pleated skirt fell forward, enough to reveal the beautiful bronze curves of her legs.

Ten thousand years ago, Quinn's primitive male ancestor would have simply reached over and grabbed. Such a woman would be a prize possession, one to keep for an extended period of time.

The primitive urge was every bit as strong now, but the bonds of civilization directed Quinn to restrain himself and politely avert his gaze. He looked down, but that was of little help, as he saw golden calf muscles bulging from feet atop black stiletto-heeled shoes, and, hey, those long legs went all the way down to the ground, didn't they? Only athletes had legs like that. Maybe she was a runner. Or a soccer player. Or—

"Are you a dancer?" Quinn sat back in his chair, pushing its back against the wall, providing a little more gentlemanly space between the two of them. He had changed his mind about conversation. A little idle chit-chat would kill time and help him blend in with the bar crowd.

"Oh!" The waitress stood up straight, realizing what had happened. Embarrassed at her exposure, she modestly straightened her skirt and top, making sure everything was back in place. Quinn gazed at his beer.

The waitress secured the bar rag and old beer bottle to the tray with one hand and put her other hand on her hip. She tossed her mane of hair over one shoulder, and looked warily at Quinn.

"I am a dancer." She hesitated, on guard against the impertinent stranger. "Why?"

"Because you're in such great shape." He gave her a reassuring smile. "Only dancers or athletes stay so fit. And your poise is that of a dancer."

Her body language relaxed. "I dance here in the hotel showroom." There was a pause as she gave him an appraising glance, then a note of pride in her voice. "I am in the weekend revue. You would like to come see the show, maybe?"

"I'd love to, but I'm leaving tonight." Quinn glanced at his watch. He had more time to kill. "I'd like to hear more about your dancing, though. I imagine you're quite passionate about it."

She looked around the room and, deciding she had time to talk, leaned against the table. "It is only part-time. Two nights a week. A nice little show for the *turistas*. It has a little of everything—salsa, tango, samba. Waiting tables, that is what pays my bills. But you are right, *señor*. Someday I hope to make it my career. My dream is to go to New York and, I think you say, go for it?"

"I don't know anything about dance, but I imagine that's the place."

"Ah!" The brown eyes flashed. "To see Broadway, to audition for the shows. And to audition for the great schools, like Ailey, Juilliard. I took ballet as a child, so maybe I get in. Already I reach the limit of what I can do here in this small town. I would be happy to be in any show in New York."

"You let me know when you're there, and I will come watch you dance." Quinn extended his hand. "I'm Michael."

"Gabriella." She clasped his hand.

Their hands stayed clasped a bit longer than normal for an introduction. As Quinn continued to make small talk with the girl, he settled back in his chair and took her in.

She was tall, maybe five foot eight. About twenty, twenty-one. The thick black hair hung straight down almost to her waist. She had a figure that made Quinn's heart pound. And her face, while a bit angular for some men, had a natural look he found appealing.

She was, as beautiful Mexican women often are, an ethnic mix—*mestizo*, was that still the word? The olive skin, the narrow European-looking nose, the full lips—those came from the Spanish empire, from some fair-skinned *conquistador* marrying a native girl long ago. But the high cheekbones, the rather square jawline, and, most of all, the fiery glint in the dark-almond eyes—those were Aztec.

Her shortie top left her very slim waist exposed, and the pleated black skirt barely reached the top of her muscular thighs. In bed, this woman would be an animal. Quinn was wondering if he could reach both hands around her waist when he realized he was being asked a question.

"… should go check my other tables. Where are you from? Maybe I'll see you around."

"California. Not too far." What to say next? "We could get together when you make that trip to New York," he finished lamely.

At the remark her face fell. Had he unwittingly struck a nerve? "That is still a dream. I'm just sort of getting by, I think you say? You know, making just enough to pay my bills. I'm embarrassed to say this, but I've never been to the United States. I've never even been outside Mexico. So, my new friend Michael, yes, New York. Someday."

"You are on your own, then?"

"For a long time."

"Same here. I like the freedom. But I know what you mean. It's not always the easiest path to where you want to go."

She hesitated, then leaned down and in. Her hair brushed his arm as her face moved close. The dark brown eyes searched his.

"Do you ever feel, sort of, trapped? That life, it is OK, you know, but that you are just on a, I think you call it, a treadmill. Do you ever feel like you want to, you know, escape? Just break out?"

She stood up and tilted her head back, awaiting his reply with a kind of dignity that came from pouring out her heart. When no reply came she turned sideways, legs slightly apart, as if, now that she had opened up, she was daring this brash *gringo* to hurry up and make his evasive, non-committal, conversation-ending reply, so that she could walk away and go back to work.

Her honesty reflected a vitality that embraced life. And her body language said that she had just thrown down some sort of gauntlet. Yes, that was it. She had just offered him a smoldering, sexual *challenge*.

"I know exactly what you mean, Gabriella." Quinn grabbed a cocktail napkin and wrote down the number of his disposable cell phone. The number would no longer exist after tonight, and thus wouldn't compromise his mission.

"Here's my cell number. I'm also writing down the name of the hotel where I'm staying. It's about two hours north of here, not too far from the border. I'm busy with work this evening, but should be back by midnight. If you'd like to break out of here, text me after midnight from the bar at my hotel, and I'll meet you there. After tonight I've got a few days off. And New York is only a five-hour flight away."

Gabriella raised her eyebrows, as if wondering whether this man was serious. Then, with a what-do-I-have-to-lose shrug, she picked up the cocktail napkin and tucked it into her skirt pocket.

She turned away, about to say good-bye, when a thunderous *boom* sounded in the distance. Heads perked up all around the bar as glassware rattled on shelves and the bottle of beer on Quinn's table vibrated. The noisy buzz of the crowd faded away.

"What was that?" said Gabriella.

• • •

Washington, D.C.

The Mexican official from the *Secretaria de Relaciones Exteriores* no longer looked cool and comfortable. His brow furrowed as he leaned forward in his chair, and he let out an exasperated sigh as he turned a page of the thick document lying on the conference table.

"This document, Mr. Jenkins, it could have been sent to us digitally. We could have discussed it over the phone. Why did your colleagues at the Department of State insist that it be reviewed in a face-to-face meeting?"

"For security reasons, Mr. Hernandez. That is all we are able to say." Jenkins put a polite smile on his face.

"I'm sorry for the inconvenience. Shall we move on to the next page? I believe it is number 138."

The Mexican official frowned. "Why is it necessary to review each page? Why not an executive summary? So far I see nothing new here. No new facts at all regarding this American."

"It was at the request of members of Congress, sir. Some representatives have introduced legislation that would suspend all foreign aid to your country until there has been marked improvement in the issues of crime and border security that are so serious that they now impact the United States. We do appreciate your cooperation."

The Mexican official muttered under his breath in Spanish, then glanced at the flashing blue screen of his vibrating cell phone. He answered the phone curtly, spoke commandingly in rapid Spanish, then stopped in mid-sentence. His demeanor changed to that of a man now taking orders. His eyes widened as he tapped keys on his laptop and looked at the screen.

The laptop was positioned so that Jenkins could also see the screen. The full screen showed a live, breaking-news broadcast from a Mexican television station.

Most of the screen showed helicopter footage of a huge fire, with yellow-orange flames leaping high in the air and billowing clouds of reddish-brown smoke. This video alternated with helicopter footage of an entirely different scene, one of Mexican citizens evacuating a small town. The video showed the panicked citizenry clogging the streets as they fled by car and truck, by bicycle and by foot, trying to escape the billowing clouds in the sky above them. There were a few Mexican police cars about, their flashing red and blue lights rendering some semblance of order to the chaos.

In the lower right-hand corner of the screen, a box showed an attractive dark-haired female news anchor, but the laptop sound was turned off. At the bottom of the screen, a scroll with bold white capital letters summarized the breaking news, and Jenkins was able to translate the scrolling Spanish sentence fragments.

MASSIVE EXPLOSION AT CHEMICAL FOOD-PROCESSING PLANT ... JUST OUTSIDE TOWN OF PUEBLO DE PESCADO ... LARGE QUANTITIES OF NITRIC ACID ACCIDENTALLY POURED INTO TANKS CONTAINING SODIUM HYDROXIDE ... CHEMICAL REACTION PRODUCED TOXIC GASES WHICH ARE EXTREMELY DANGEROUS IF ANY CONTACT WITH THE HUMAN BODY ... PLANT SENSOR SYSTEM DETECTED EXPLOSION, SENT ALARM SIGNAL ORDERING EVACUATION ... LARGE CLOUDS OF GASES SPREAD RAPIDLY BY WINDS ... ALL EMPLOYEES OF ADJACENT FACILITIES, INCLUDING PRISIÓN FEDERAL, ORDERED TO IMMEDIATELY EVACUATE VICINITY ... RISK ZONE EXTENDED TO INCLUDE TOWN OF PUEBLO DE PESCADO ... SPECIALIST TEAMS WITH HAZMAT SUITS EXPECTED TO ARRIVE BY LATE EVENING.

"Madre de Dios." The Mexican official spoke softly as he stared at the screen.

Jenkins raised his eyebrows in an expression of polite concern. "Is something wrong?"

• • •

Pueblo de Pescado,
Mexico

The 500cc dirt bike shot down the alley, then slowed as it turned onto the boulevard.

The street was already a gridlock of cars and trucks, the smoky air filled with a chorus of car horns and angry yells. Quinn had expected this. He flicked the bike onto the sidewalk.

He snaked around startled pedestrians, guiding the bike through whatever pockets of space opened up in front of him, alternating between the street curbside and the sidewalk. Word of the evacuation had spread quickly, and people were spilling out from buildings and stores.

He made his way through city blocks that were a blur of jabbering faces, then turned into an alley that he had memorized as part of his escape route. The alley was blessedly empty, and led him to a series of quiet side streets. A final turn, and then he was on the highway leading to the *Prisión.*

Now he was ahead of the fleeing populace, and traffic on the highway was light. The bike whined as he pushed it to seventy, then eighty, and suddenly the turn-off for the prison loomed up on his right. He slowed for the curving exit ramp, then brought the bike onto the long driveway that led only to the prison.

Ahead of him the entrance came into view. The text he had received confirmed that the gate was jammed open and the yards and watchtowers empty. All of the guards and employees had fled immediately upon hearing the evacuation order, leaving the prisoners behind. He slowed the bike to a crawl as he rode through the entrance, one hand on his holstered 9mm.

With the prison adjacent to the chemical plant, smoke was everywhere, and several times thicker than in town. Reddish-brown haze hung down to the ground, so dense it partially obscured the buildings.

The compound was a fire-and-brimstone hell, the *guarida del diablo*. The dimmed sun turned the day into a sulphurous twilight, with everything covered in soot. The alarm horns had finished, and the only noise was the dull rumble of the prisoners trapped in their cells, their shouting muffled by thick concrete walls.

Quinn guided the bike through the haze to the side entrance of the solitary building. He dismounted, chained the bike to one of the bars on the window next to the entry door, and clipped the key ring to his belt.

The smoke stung his eyes and irritated his lungs. He drew his 9mm and approached the open entry door from the side, making sure it was clear. As he entered the building the rumble of the prisoners became a roar.

The one-story building stank of urine and vomit, and the prisoners that saw Quinn reached through the bars and shouted for help. He ignored them and jogged down to the third cell on his right.

Something was wrong.

This man in the filthy cell didn't look like the Devereaux in the photograph. The gaunt figure in a dirty T-shirt and khakis, sitting forlornly on the bunk, resembled a picture from a concentration camp. His skin was pale and the eyes had a hollow, deep-set stare.

Quinn examined the facial features. "Bobby Devereaux?"

"No, sir. I'm—hold on." The man stood and moved forward as far as the ankle chains padlocked to his bunk would allow. "Who the hell are you?"

"What's your birthday, Devereaux?" The facial structure and eye color matched, but Quinn needed to be sure.

"November twelfth."

"Good answer. And your mother's maiden name."

"Long. You special ops?"

"Affirmative, Devereaux. Here to get you out. Stand back, I'm going to use a lock-popper."

The chains clanked as Devereaux retreated to the rear corner of his bunk. He watched Quinn attach the foot-long adhesive strip to the cell door lock, then step back. Both men turned their heads away, and with a *bang* the breaching charge blew the door open.

"What the hell's goin' on outside?" Devereaux's words tumbled out. "Everyone's yellin' 'bout some explosion at the chemical plant next door. Sayin' that clouds of toxic smoke are floatin' over that are gonna kill us all, that the goddam coward guards left us here to die."

"Hold up your wrists." Quinn took a pair of bolt-cutters out of his backpack and cut away the man's handcuffs. "The smoke clouds are all a fake. A ruse to get you out of here. Tell you more later." He glanced at the bruises and welts on the prisoner's face and arms, then knelt down and cut away the ankle chains. "Can you walk?"

"I'll run like a damn jackrabbit to get outta here."

"Follow me."

Quinn jogged back toward the open doorway. So far so good. He had his hands on the key ring on his belt and had just passed from the dark building's doorway into the outdoors when an arm grabbed him around the neck and then shoved him downward.

He stumbled on the porch step and fell forward. As he brought his arms up to break his fall, he saw the steel blade of the shiv in the man's other hand coming at him, going for his throat. He grabbed the man's knife hand with both hands and twisted hard to the right, forcing the man to fall down with him or have his wrist broken.

Both men toppled to the dirt. The man was choking him with the arm around his neck, but Quinn kept a tight grip on the man's knife hand and twisted it further until the wrist broke with an audible *snap*.

The man screamed and let go of the knife. A sharp elbow jab to the man's throat, and the scream became choking sounds.

Quinn grabbed the knife and rolled over in the dirt until he was clear. His attacker, a shirtless Mexican prisoner with an upper body covered in gang tattoos, writhed in the dirt, his hand on his throat. A few yards away, Devereaux scuffled in the dirt with another prisoner, also a tattooed gangbanger. Quinn sprang to his feet and drew his 9mm, looking for a clean shot.

The prisoner, seeing the gun trained on him, put Devereaux in a chokehold and dragged him to his feet in front of him, blocking Quinn's shot. The gangbanger brought his other arm up and held the point of his shiv blade against Devereaux's throat. He stepped back, facing off against Quinn.

"Las llaves! Ahora!" The prisoner threatened with a slicing motion across Devereaux's throat.

"Sí, sí, no problema." Quinn grabbed his key ring and, moving slowly and deliberately, unclipped it from his belt.

Devereaux stood still, the knifepoint pressed tight against his throat. He made eye contact with Quinn, then glanced at both of his hands.

Devereaux's left hand held a fistful of dirt, and his right forearm had moved up until it was behind, but not touching, the forearm of the man's knife hand. Quinn looked back at Devereaux and nodded.

"Sí, sí, amigo, you can have the motorcycle keys." Quinn held the key ring in front of him and jangled the keys. "See? Here they are. You can have the keys right *now."*

He tossed the keys directly into the gangbanger's face.

At the same time, Devereaux shoved the man's knife arm forward and rubbed his fistful of dirt in the man's eyes. The man yelled as Devereaux lifted both arms up, dropped down, and rolled away.

Quinn fired two rounds into the gangbanger's bare chest and another to the head. The man crumpled to the ground, making gurgling noises. Quinn walked over, placed the barrel of his 9mm against the center of the man's forehead, and fired another round. The man stopped making noise and lay still.

The gangbanger with the broken wrist had pushed himself up on one arm, crawling toward the dead man's knife. Quinn turned and fired three quick rounds. The gangbanger rolled onto his back and lay there motionless, blood streaking his face.

Quinn picked up the key ring, unchained the bike, straddled it and fired it up. Devereaux climbed on the rear seat.

"Hold on," Quinn shouted over the whine of the engine. He pointed to dark shapes moving in the haze around other buildings. Prisoners were pouring out of the building exits. "The way out's going to get busy."

He pulled the bike out of the courtyard and rounded the corner of the solitary building, heading toward the entrance. Ahead of him the prison yards that had been empty when he rode in now looked like a village of the damned.

Ghostly human shapes were everywhere, appearing and then disappearing into the thick smoke as panicked prisoners fled in all directions. Screams and shrieks echoed off the abandoned buildings. Quinn threaded the bike around the shadowy shapes, slowing when he had to, speeding up when he hit a patch of empty asphalt.

He swerved hard to the left as a bottle smashed to the ground in front of them, showering them in shards of glass. The bike shuddered as a prisoner grabbed Devereaux's leg, trying to knock them over. Devereaux grunted and kicked out hard, and the prisoner doubled over, squealing in pain as the bike shot forward.

Now the entrance was visible ahead. Prisoners ran at them from all sides, trying to cut them off. Quinn jerked the bike right, left, right, inches beyond a blur of grasping hands and shouting faces.

The bike engine screamed as they shot through the open gate and onto the long driveway. Bottles crashed into the asphalt behind them, and then the yells of the prisoners faded into the background.

At the highway Quinn slowed and turned left, away from town. The road ahead looked empty. The citizens of Pueblo de Pescado had fled in the other direction, towards the closest city.

Now for the homestretch. Quinn twisted the throttle, and the bike tore down the blacktop. The desert became an endless blur, and ahead of them the sun was a copper-colored streak on the horizon. The only sounds were the whine of the engine and the roar of the wind.

By the time Quinn pulled over and turned off the highway into the desert, night had fallen. In the darkness he slowed their speed to twenty, using the headlight to guide the bike over undulating sand hills punctuated by shrubs of mesquite and creosote. About a half hour in he stopped, checked the GPS on his cell phone, and killed the engine.

"OK, Bobby, here's where we dismount and stretch our legs. We're almost home." As he walked, he tapped the keys on his phone and put it on speaker.

"This is Spartan 33, Atlas 11 come in."

"Go ahead, Spartan 33," crackled a voice on the speaker.

"Atlas 11, I have Bulls-eye in position. Repeat, have Bulls-eye in position."

"Spartan 33, copy, we are ten minutes out. Mark position to identify."

Quinn removed a rectangular object the size of a flashlight from his backpack, walked several yards out, and placed it on a level patch of sand with its lens facing up.

"Atlas 11, this is Spartan 33, position marked by IR strobe, ready for extract."

"Spartan 33, copy, on our way."

Devereaux watched with interest. "A helo?"

Quinn pointed. "From behind those hills."

Devereaux gave a long sigh of relief. He extended his hand. "I don't believe I got your name."

"Michael Quinn." They shook hands.

"That was a hell of a stunt you pulled off back there, Michael. What'd you rig up at that plant, smoke bombs?"

"In large quantities, so the winds would spread the smoke. For the explosion, I used C4 to blow up an empty warehouse. Accelerant for the fire."

"And that alarm?"

"Cyberintel hacked into the plant's computer system to set off the toxic-gas alarm and evacuation order. By now the hazmat teams are probably at the plant, surprised to find there were never toxic gases of any kind."

"Appreciate you savin' my ass. Things were lookin' a bit grim back there." He coughed, a racking cough that shook his upper body, and spat in the sand.

Quinn removed two water bottles from the bike's saddlebag and handed one to Devereaux. He had liked the man instinctively. Now it looked like he wanted to talk, and there was time. "The SEALs weren't about to let anything happen to one of their best men. You've been through quite a bit, Bobby. Any plans for when you get home?"

Devereaux took a long drink from the bottle and looked out at the stars. His gaunt face was pensive.

"Had plenty of time to think 'bout that." He took another drink.

"Gotta girl back home. Been goin' together three years now. Cute little thing, a runner. I can see her bouncing blond ponytail now. Gotta good job, too, a physical therapist.

"She's been patient, waitin' for me. And I been put-tin' her off, 'cause of my work, me being gone so much. You know how it is.

"Lotta guys lose their girlfriends, even their wives, 'cause of that. It seems like you're overseas most all the time, and then, even when you're back home, in your mind you're still gone.

"That ain't gonna happen to me. Two months was-tin' away in that hellhole of a cell taught me that you never know when your own number's gonna come up. We're only here for a while, y'know?"

Devereaux finished the last of his water and gazed at something far away.

"So, when I get home I'm gonna grab this girl and pop the question. And if she'll have me, I ain't never lettin' her go."

For a moment the men stood in silence. The night-time desert was a different world from the smoky inferno of the day. The bright moon cast its lumines-cence across endless rippled sand. Stars glittered qui-etly against a jet-black sky.

Devereaux glanced at Quinn. "What about you? You got someone special?"

Before Quinn could reply, a rhythmic thumping noise sliced through the air.

The men searched the sky for the source of the noise.

Thunderous rotor beats echoed as the dark silhou-ette of the Blackhawk helicopter rose up from behind the hills. Quinn put on his night-vision goggles and pointed out to Devereaux where the silhouette of the helicopter blotted out a patch of stars.

The chopper flew towards them, then hovered over a flat stretch of desert. The rotor wash kicked up a brief whirling sandstorm as the helo landed.

Quinn motioned for Devereaux to climb back on the bike. He kept it in first gear as he eased it over to the waiting Blackhawk. When they were a few yards away, the passenger door opened.

He stopped the bike and turned to Devereaux. "The pilots will take over from here. They'll ID you, to make sure who you are. Then the chopper will take you to a hospital in Camp Pendleton. They'll make sure you're OK, debrief you, get some food in you, and then get you home."

"You ain't comin'?" Devereaux looked surprised as he dismounted.

"Bobby, after what went down today, I can't be seen within a hundred miles of you. But I've got a feeling our paths will cross again."

"I hope so. Looks like things ain't dull when you're around."

Quinn's disposable cell phone beeped in his back pocket. He fished the phone out and glanced at the flashing blue screen.

I am here. Gabriella. read the simple text message.

"And my day's not quite over." Quinn tapped the keys and sent his reply.

"I've got one more stop to make tonight."

For more works by the author visit
www.kevinscottolson.com